YOU CHOOSE
BOOKS

CAN YOU SURVIVE A
VIRUS OUTBREAK?

An Interactive Doomsday Adventure

by MATT DOE...

illustrated b...

D1078141

tree
publishers for children

Raintree is an imprint of Capstone Global Library Limited, a company incorporated in England and Wales having its registered office at 7 Pilgrim Street, London, EC4V 6LB – Registered company number: 6695582

www.raintree.co.uk
myorders@raintree.co.uk

Editorial Credits
Anthony Wacholtz, editor; Bobbie Nuytten, designer;
Wanda Winch, media researcher; Kathy McColley, production specialist;
Nathan Gassman, creative director
Printed and bound in China.

ISBN 978 1 4747 0706 0
19 18 17 16 15
10 9 8 7 6 5 4 3 2 1

British Library Cataloguing in Publication Data
A full catalogue record for this book is available from the British Library.

Acknowledgements
Getty Images: DEA/De Agostini/G. DAGLI ORTI, 102; Shutterstock: AlexVector, background (throughout), Ihor Pasternak, 107 (left), Irina_QQQ, design element, Mtsaride, 107 (right), tomwa, 106, tuulijumala, 111

Every effort has been made to contact copyright holders of material reproduced in this book. Any omissions will be rectified in subsequent printings if notice is given to the publisher.

CONTENTS

ABOUT YOUR
ADVENTURE

You are living through a dark and dangerous time in the near future of humanity. A terrible new virus is about to wreak havoc on the world's population. How will you survive? Start off by turning the page, then follow the directions at the bottom of each page. The choices you make will change the outcome of your story. After you finish one path, go back and read the others to see how other choices would have changed your fate. Do you have what it takes to survive doomsday?

YOU CHOOSE the path you take through a Virus Outbreak.

BLOOD FEVER

You can barely contain your excitement as you gaze out of the window of your aeroplane seat. You fidget in your seat, eager for the flight to reach its destination, Port au Prince, Haiti. You smirk, knowing your classmates are back at home, sitting in a maths lesson right now. But you're getting a head start on the Easter holidays – a two-week visit to Haiti to visit your sister Tara. She's a medical student, volunteering in a small village in the poverty-stricken nation of Haiti.

After you land, you check your phone. There's a text from Tara: *Running late. Sry!*

Great, you think with a groan. You find a seat and watch people come and go. It's a bustling airport. People are scrambling to queue up at the ticket and check-in desks.

Turn the page

A man in a suit and tie sitting next to you is reading the sport section of a newspaper. The front page sits on the spare seat between you.

"Do you mind if I read this?" you ask.

He shrugs and hands you the paper. "Be my guest. But there's not much in here for a kid. Terrorist attacks in South Asia, stock market crashing, a nasty virus spreading outside Santo Domingo. Adult stuff. Might be a crossword puzzle in the back, though."

You mutter a "thank you" and try not to roll your eyes. You may still be a teenager, but that doesn't mean you're not interested in current affairs. You glance at every story. The outbreak in Santo Domingo – the media is calling it Blood Fever – catches your attention. Santo Domingo is the capital of the Dominican Republic, a nation that shares the island of Hispaniola with Haiti. Nobody seems to know where the outbreak came from. Scary stuff, but you're sure that doctors will get it under control. After all, this is the 21st century.

An hour passes, then two. Suddenly you notice that the queues for customs are empty. People coming and going seem agitated. Several airport employees rush by, speaking loudly.

"Parlez-vous anglais?" you ask a woman at a help desk. You're learning French at school, but you're not ready for a full conversation with a native speaker.

"Oui," she answers. "I speak English."

"What's going on?" you ask.

"It's Blood Fever. They've found some cases here in Haiti."

Before you can reply, you hear someone calling your name. It's Tara! She rushes over and wraps you up in a giant hug.

"So sorry to be late," Tara says. "One of my patients took a bad turn. Had to get her stable before I left."

"It's not Blood Fever, is it?" you ask nervously.

"No, no. It couldn't be. Probably just a flu bug."

Turn the page

"They say that the virus has spread to Haiti," you tell Tara.

"Really? News travels slowly out here, but that's surprising. We knew it would spread. But so quickly?"

Over Tara's shoulder, you see the queues for tickets and check-in growing. People are pushing and shoving, trying to move to the front.

"Perhaps you being here isn't such a good idea," Tara says. "We should get you on a flight home."

Your heart sinks. You've been looking forward to this trip for months.

"You're staying, aren't you?" you ask.

"Of course. If there's an outbreak, they'll need all the help they can get."

Going home would probably be the wise decision. But you can't bear the thought of turning around and getting right back on a plane.

To stay with Tara, go to page 11.
To get in the queue to buy a ticket home, turn to page 61.

"If you're staying, I'm staying," you tell Tara, putting your rucksack over your shoulder.

"All right then," she says. "Let's get going. We've got a two-hour drive ahead of us."

You climb into Tara's small rental car. You leave the sprawling terraces of Port au Prince behind and trace the coast along the motorway. Soon you turn north onto a small dirt road, rumbling up steep terrain to a little village.

"That's where we're working," Tara says, pointing to a small group of tents. "We live in a small barracks on the other side of the village. Our main job is to vaccinate children against diseases – measles, whooping cough, the usual suspects. But we also help with locals who need care."

Tara parks the car and leads you through the village. The homes are rundown, and animals roam through the streets. But the people are friendly. They greet you as you pass by, offering smiles and waves.

Turn the page

"Here we are," she says, gesturing you into the crude field hospital they've set up. "I'll get you settled into your barrack in a moment. Just want to check on Maria first. She's the patient I was looking after earlier."

Several people lie on camp beds. One has a broken arm. Another is bent over with a rattling cough. Maria is at the back, separated from the rest with plastic sheets. You watch from outside as Tara steps in and slips on gloves and a mask. Maria is a young woman, perhaps 25 years old. Her skin is pale and waxy, and she seems barely conscious. Tara rests her hand on Maria's forehead and frowns.

"She's burning up," Tara tells Jim, one of the other medical students.

"I know," he says. "We can't seem to control the fever. And it gets worse." Jim lifts the sheet and points to a bright red rash of tiny blood blisters covering Maria's chest and shoulders.

Tara flinches. "How ... it can't be here already."

Turn the page

Jim shakes his head. "I don't understand it either. But there's no doubt. Blood Fever is here, and we're not ready for it. No one is."

Tara spends several more minutes talking to Jim. Then she peels off her gloves and mask and joins you outside. "Look," she says. "I'm not sure having you here is a great idea. I didn't know the virus would be here so soon. I think it's best if you keep your distance."

"Please," you beg. "I want to help. It's why I came!"

Tara sighs. She's never been able to say no to you. "Okay, look. If you come back to the hospital with me, you wear gloves and a mask at all times. And no direct contact with patients. Or … I have another way you can help. Jim has been studying the local herbs here. You could go out and collect some that have immune-boosting properties. They might just give us the edge against this virus."

To return to the hospital with Tara, go to page 15.
To talk to Jim and gather herbs, turn to page 16.

"I want to see you in action," you tell Tara.

Tara grins. "Okay, then," she says, handing you a surgical mask. "Whenever you're near the hospital, wear this mask. The virus is extremely contagious."

After a quick tour of the hospital, Tara puts you to work. It's not quite what you had imagined. Instead of drawing blood or taking temperatures, you're fetching food and water, and changing beds.

The cases of Blood Fever start as a trickle. But soon they come more rapidly. After two days there are six cases. After three, the number swells to seventeen. Maria drifts in and out of consciousness. She doesn't seem to be improving.

The next day, Jim speaks up at breakfast. "It's getting worse," he says. "The hospitals in Port au Prince are overrun. There are dead in the streets, and the airport is closed. Before things get worse, we need supplies. Today might be our last chance if things continue to fall apart."

To go to Port au Prince with Jim, turn to page 18.
To stay behind and help with the patients, turn to page 25.

You catch Jim just as he's leaving the hospital. He looks exhausted. "Two more cases came in last night, and Maria is getting worse by the hour," he tells you as you walk together. "It's spreading much faster than anyone expected. Things are going to get really bad around here. It might be time for you to leave."

"Nah," you tell him with a grin. "I want to help. Tara thought you might put me to work gathering herbs."

"The locals swear by them," Jim says. "There's an old woman a few villages north who can name every plant that grows here. I spent a few days with her and learned some valuable things. I'm not sure how much herbs really help, but we've got precious little medicine here. It's better than nothing."

You walk together as Jim tells you what to look for. Sarsaparilla root … mint leaves … bitterwood bark … the list goes on. He takes a book from his bunk. It's packed with photos of native plants. "Find what you can," Jim says.

You head north-east of the village. You spend your day creeping through forests, scrambling over rocks and digging out roots. Before you realize how late it is, the sun is setting. You'd better get back while you've still got some light. Grasping your bag loaded with leaves, bark and roots, you turn to head back to the village.

You take a sharp breath and swallow a scream. Someone is watching you! The figure is stooped, and cloaked in robes. Your heart races.

To turn and run, turn to page 20.
To approach the stranger, turn to page 22.

The rusty old Jeep rumbles down the motorway. The road is almost deserted. In the distance, you see smoke rising above the trees. You don't want to know what's burning.

The smell hits you as you arrive at the outer limits of the city. It instantly takes you back to the day when you found a dead fox in your garden.

"There's a supermarket up ahead," he says, turning the Jeep down a side street. A thin man waves at you from the other side of the street, and starts stumbling in your direction. He shouts to you in a raspy voice. The man's face is flushed and marked with small blisters.

"He's asking us for help," Jim says, shaking his head. "But he's ill. There's no telling what he might do."

The man continues to shout to you urgently. He seems desperate.

To let the man approach, turn to page 29.
To ask Jim to get you out of there, turn to page 32.

19

As fast as you can, you turn and dart off into the woods. You run, tree branches slapping your face, until your foot slips on a loose rock. Your ankle twists, and you shout out as you crumple to the ground. Your bag of herbs sprawls out before you, its contents spread across the ground.

Your ankle throbs, but it's not broken. You look around as you catch your breath. There's nobody else here. But you don't recognize the landscape. You're at the base of a rocky hill. The sun has almost completely set. Quickly, you get your bearings. "West is that way," you mumble to yourself.

There's not much light left, and you'll be limping, so time is critical. You grab a few of the herbs lying near by, but end up leaving most of them where they lie. You know as long as you move west, you'll hit the little dirt road that leads to the village.

As you limp along, the sky darkens overhead. As the air cools, a swarm of mosquitoes buzz around you. You swat and slap as you move, but the bugs are relentless. By the time you find the dirt road and follow it back to the village, you're covered in itchy bites.

"Thank goodness!" Tara cries as you limp into town. "What happened to you?"

Others gather around as you tell your tale. You notice Jim smirking in the background.

"That sounds like Leila," Jim says. "She's the woman I was telling you about. The locals call her a leaf doctor. She was probably gathering herbs, like you were."

You groan, feeling silly for running away from an old woman. "I'll go back out tomorrow," you tell Jim. "Now I know what I'm looking for."

You have a restless night, scratching at all of your insect bites. You roll out of bed at sunrise, but you feel terrible. Your stomach is churning, and you're sweating.

To report to the hospital, turn to page 34.
To go out to collect herbs, turn to page 39.

"Bonjour," you say, stepping forward. "Hello?"

The stranger straightens and peels back a hood. It's an old woman. A bag is slung over her shoulder. She smiles at you.

She doesn't speak English, but your French is just good enough to keep a conversation going. Her name is Leila, and she's gathering herbs, just like you are. It doesn't take long before you realize she's the woman Jim told you about – a "leaf doctor".

She waves you over. She wants you to come with her. You look back towards the village and see the sun is already beginning to set. Tara will be worried, but you feel like you should go with her.

You spend the night in Leila's small hut. It's an amazing experience. Carefully, step-by-step, Leila shows you how to make a tea from nearly a dozen local herbs. She boils water in a small pot, carefully adding herbs as she goes. Finally, she hands you a steaming cup.

Turn the page

You drink it. It's bitter, but you swallow down every last drop. Leila smiles and pats your head.

In the morning, you head back. Your bag is packed with all of the herbs you need to make Leila's tea. You follow the small dirt road back to the village. The hike takes more than an hour, but you feel energized.

Tara rushes up and wraps you in a bear hug as you enter the village. "Don't ever do that again!" she scolds.

You tell everyone your tale and show them the herbs Leila gave you. "There's not a sick person in her whole village," you explain. Some of the medical students seem sceptical. You know that many doctors have a low opinion of herbal treatments. "What harm is there in trying?" you ask.

Soon you're at work brewing Leila's tea, carefully following the steps she taught you. You've got enough for about 20 people. But who would benefit most from drinking it, the healthy or the sick?

To give the tea to the students and other healthy people in the village, turn to page 43.
To give the tea to the sick patients, turn to page 47.

The hospital is filling at an alarming rate. Your day is spent washing soiled bedsheets, carrying water from the well to the hospital and doing anything you can to be useful. The work is hard, and by evening you're exhausted. But it feels good to make a difference.

As the sun sets, that feeling quickly fades. Jim hasn't returned from his supply run. "It's not like him," Tara says, wringing her hands. "I can't imagine he would have just abandoned us."

You're not sure what to say. Jim could be in trouble. His Jeep could have broken down. He could have fallen ill – or worse.

Turn the page

"I think I should go after him," Tara says. "One of the villagers has a motorbike that I'm sure I could use. But with Jim gone, they can't spare any help at the hospital. We're getting more and more patients, and the fever is already more than we can handle."

She's distraught. You have a feeling that you're never going to see Jim again, one way or the other. But you hate seeing Tara like this. Maybe you could give her some peace of mind by looking for Jim yourself. The village can do without you for a day, but the people need Tara.

To convince Tara you are both needed at the hospital,
turn to page 28.
To volunteer to take the motorbike into Port au Prince
to look for Jim, turn to page 58.

"If he's gone, he's gone," you tell Tara with a hug. "Even if you knew where he was going, the odds of finding him are pretty low. We just have to wait. In the meantime, we can try to help these people."

Tara sighs with tears in her eyes. She knows you're right. The days stretch on, and the sick continue to come in. There's been no sign of Jim. You hope he found a safe place, even if you don't really believe it.

Within a week, the hospital is overflowing. You wash your hands several times every hour and wear a mask and gloves. You minimize close contact with anyone – including Tara. But it's not enough. Just 10 days after you arrived in Haiti, you wake up in the morning feeling ill. You rush outside and vomit, followed by 10 minutes of painful dry heaves.

You close your eyes and rest for a moment. You try to convince yourself it's just the flu or something you ate. But you recognize the symptoms of Blood Fever. It's time to break the bad news to Tara.

Turn to page 50.

"The whole reason we came to Haiti was to help, wasn't it?" you say before Jim can drive away. He closes his eyes and slumps his shoulders.

"You're right. Okay, let's do what we can."

The sick man appears to be in his thirties, but the fever has hit him hard. His skin sags off his arms and dark circles hang under his eyes. His half-panicked speech is too rapid for you to follow, but Jim is fluent in French. They speak for several moments before Jim turns to you.

"His wife has died, and his child is sick. He's begging for us to help him."

You both agree you'll do what you can. The man leads you to his nearby home – a small shack with a dirt floor. You enter and wince. The smell of death here is overwhelming.

Turn the page

The child – a young boy, perhaps four years old – lies on a pile of blankets on the floor. Jim places his hand on the child's forehead. "He's burning up," he whispers. "His fever is advanced. There's nothing we can do."

As the three of you stand over the boy, the father begins to hack and cough. When he pulls his hand away from his mouth, it's covered in blood and mucus. You feel helpless.

Jim reaches into his rucksack. He pulls out a water bottle, presses it into the man's hand and walks back outside. You follow him out.

"They're dying and you give them water?"

Jim shrugs. "What else could I do? They're both desperately dehydrated. I told him that it was medicine."

"Do we go to the market then?"

"No," Jim says, shaking his head. "There's nothing there. He told me that all the supplies went days ago."

It's a sombre ride back to the village. The sun is setting as you pull up. Tara rushes out and wraps you up in a big hug. "I was so worried," she says. There's a tear on her cheek.

As bad as things seem now, they only get worse. Two patients died while you were away. The next day, three more join them. You help Jim and some others to dig graves. By the end of the day, you're completely exhausted and drenched in sweat. You sit down for some supper with the rest, but you just can't bring yourself to eat anything.

That night, you can't sleep. Your stomach churns and grumbles. Around midnight, you step outside and vomit violently onto the ground. You crouch there a moment, shivering, knowing what this means. You've caught Blood Fever. And there's no cure.

Turn to page 50.

As the man draws near, it becomes clear that he's reached an advanced state of infection. Before he can get to your Jeep, he doubles over in a fit of coughing. His hands are covered in blood. He's well beyond your help.

"Go," you say quietly. "We can't help him, Jim. We have to go."

The man slumps to the ground as you drive off. Your heart sinks as you watch him collapse. But you had no choice.

Finally you arrive at your destination. Jim curses as he surveys the scene. The doors have been torn off the hinges. Broken shelves and shredded food packaging litter the car park. Several young men stand near to the entrance, fixing you both with hard gazes.

"It might not be empty," Jim says. But neither of you really believe it.

"We have to go, Jim." The young men standing by the door have started to move in your direction. They do not look friendly. "Jim ... now, Jim!"

Finally, with a shake of his head, Jim puts the Jeep in gear and slams the accelerator. That's when you hear the shot ring out. The Jeep lurches violently to one side. "The tyres!" Jim shouts. "They're shooting at the tyres!"

Another shot rings out, and the Jeep grinds to a halt. A look over your shoulder sends a chill down your spine. They're coming for you.

"Stay calm," Jim says. "They probably only want our money and supplies."

He steps out of the Jeep, his hands in the air. Your heart is racing. The young men approaching look desperate and very threatening. You rest your hand on the door handle.

To open the door and run, turn to page 52.
To stay in the Jeep and let Jim talk to them,
turn to page 56.

Something's not right. You need to see Tara or one of the other medical students right away. You wipe the sweat off your brow and limp down to the hospital. But as you approach, a chill runs down your spine. Jim and another med student are carrying a stretcher. On it rests a slender figure, wrapped in a bedsheet. You don't have to ask. You already know – it's Maria.

Tara rushes out of the hospital and wraps you in an embrace. You hold your breath – if you've got Blood Fever, you don't want to infect Tara. "Oh, we tried," Tara says, weeping. "There just wasn't anything we could do. And the others are getting worse so quickly. There's more than a dozen now. More coming in every hour, it seems."

Turn the page

You hate to tell her, but you have no choice. You push out of her hug and take a step back. "Tara … you need to wear your mask."

"I don't understand," she says. But you can see in her face that she does. "Oh no … not you! Maybe it's something else. Something you ate."

"Maybe," you say, nodding. "But maybe not."

It doesn't take long to find out. Tara takes some blood and runs a test. It's official. You've got Blood Fever. You overhear one of the other medical students talking about the disease spreading through mosquito bites. That must be how the disease found you.

Tara is determined to get you to a proper hospital. She begs Jim to take you into Port au Prince. Reluctantly, he agrees. Within an hour, the three of you are in Jim's Jeep, rumbling down the road. The bumpy motion of the Jeep makes you feel ill. You make Jim pull over so you can vomit into a ditch.

"You're not looking too good," Jim says. You know it's true. One moment, you're burning up. The next, you've got the chills. It's a long, miserable ride. And your mood doesn't improve when you reach the city.

Port au Prince has been hit hard. Fires burn in the distance. People lie sleeping in the streets. At least you hope they're sleeping. Jim weaves through the streets of the city, finally pulling up to a large, gated building. The sign reads "*Hôpital Asile Français D'Haiti.*" Jim tells you to wait and goes inside.

Twenty minutes later, he returns to the Jeep. He slams the door shut in frustration. "They're not admitting anyone," he says. "Every bed is taken. They don't have the staff."

Turn the page

You try several other hospitals in the city, but the story is always the same. Blood Fever has overwhelmed them. And now doctors and nurses are becoming ill. There's simply nowhere to turn.

By the time the three of you return to the village, it's dark. You're exhausted and weak. It takes both Jim and Tara to help you to your bed. You notice Tara's face streaked with tears.

The virus hits you harder than most. Within a day, you're covered in painful blood blisters. You can't keep food or water down. Tara does all she can, but she never has a chance. Just eight days after your first symptom, your fever soars to 40 degrees. It's more than your body can take. You slip away into a deep darkness, one victim among millions of the terrible Blood Fever.

THE END

To follow another path, turn to page 10.
To learn more about virus outbreaks, turn to page 103.

You're determined to bring Jim the herbs he asked for. Maybe some fresh morning air will help you feel better. You take off from the village, keeping a sharp eye for what you need. Now that you've done this once before, you're confident you can get what you need and be back before the day gets too hot.

You've barely walked a kilometre before you have to stop to rest. Sweat pours down your face, and you feel your knees trembling. You drink deeply from your canteen of water, but moments later, your stomach heaves. You retch and throw it all back up.

Turn the page

Uh-oh, you think. You're beginning to realize that you're truly ill. Last night you were feeling fine, and now you can barely make yourself move. How could you have become ill so quickly?

You scratch one of your mosquito bites and your fingers come away bloody. You stare at the smear of red, and it hits you. The mosquitoes! That's how Blood Fever is spreading so quickly. The mosquitoes are carrying it! And you were bitten dozens of times. You've got to tell Tara. Maybe this information will be useful. They could set up mosquito nets ... use insect repellant ... *something*!

You stand and begin to march back to the village. But your head is swimming. Was it this way? You shake your head, trying to clear the cobwebs. No... it's that way. No...

Turn the page

Just standing makes you feel lightheaded. The darkness begins to creep in around the edges of your vision. The next thing you know, you're lying on the ground. You fainted. Your head is aching. You must have hit it on a rock. Now blood is pooling on the ground below you. Once again you retch and heave.

"Help!" you shout, but it's a feeble yell, and you're far from the village. You're dehydrated, and it's getting worse by the moment as you bleed. You can't stand without passing out, and no help is coming. You know it's a bad idea, but all you want to do is close your eyes. You fight the urge for a few moments, but it's pointless. You quickly drift off to a sleep from which you never wake.

THE END

To follow another path, turn to page 10.
To learn more about virus outbreaks, turn to page 103.

Your first instinct is to give Leila's tea to the sick. But the more you think about it, the more you're convinced it's the healthy who would benefit most. The herbs are supposed to boost the immune system. That might keep people from catching the virus in the first place.

Some of the medical students grumble about drinking a herbal tea, but a stern look from Jim is all the convincing they need. Soon all of the healthy people have had a dose. Day after day, you collect herbs and brew your tea. As you get better at finding the ingredients you need, you can make more and more. Soon you're able to brew enough so that everyone in the village has a dose every day or two.

Turn the page

The tea doesn't seem to help the sick very much. You and Tara cry together on the day that Maria finally loses her battle with the fever. Others follow. But amazingly, the number of sick all but stops growing. Over the next week, only three new cases come in.

In time, it becomes clear that you've discovered something really important. "We've got to get the word out before it's too late," Tara says. Jim heads into Port au Prince to show people how to brew the tea. Meanwhile, you and several others take the treatment from village to village.

Weeks go by. Months. On a supply run, Jim comes across an old long-range radio. You gather around with Jim, Tara and some of the others as he tunes in to a radio broadcast from the World Service.

Turn the page

" ...as the fever spreads, more and more governments are falling into chaos. Madrid lies in ruin. Los Angeles has been evacuated. China has sealed its borders. Yet there seem to be slivers of hope. New anti-viral medications are showing promise. And an explosion of herbal remedies, said to have originated out of Haitian herbal lore, have been proven effective in preventing the disease among the healthy."

Tara smiles at you. The world will never be the same. You may never see your home again. But you're among people you love here. You don't know what will happen. But you're confident that humanity will survive, and you like to think that you played some small part in the battle against Blood Fever.

THE END
To follow another path, turn to page 10.
To learn more about virus outbreaks, turn to page 103.

"There's no time to waste," you tell Tara as you bring your brew to the hospital. The first patient you go to is Maria. She's awake, but just barely. Tara holds her head up as you carefully pour the tea into her mouth.

You go from patient to patient. Some of them grimace as they drink the bitter brew. One older man smiles weakly at you and says, "Merci!"

A routine begins. In the mornings, you go out to collect the herbs you need. You brew the tea in the afternoon and bring it to the sick, but only after tasting it yourself to make sure it's right. At first, it seems to help. But the number of sick just keeps growing and growing. Within a week, the hospital is overflowing.

One day as you return from your herb collecting, you see Jim sitting with his head in his hands. You know he's got bad news.

Turn the page

"Maria passed away this morning," he tells you. But the news only gets worse from there. "And now Tara is sick. Most of the other medical students too."

Your heart sinks, but you knew this could happen. You rush to brew some tea and take Tara the first cup.

Within days, the dead are mounting too quickly to bury. The healthy drag the bodies far from the village, lay them onto huge pyres and light them on fire.

On the day Tara dies, the rattle of an old motorbike comes down the road. The village is almost deserted. You and Jim are the only healthy people left. You stay close as the rider approaches and removes his helmet.

From a distance, you exchange news. The rider, who speaks English, paints a dismal picture. "Port au Prince is all but wiped out. All of the major cities lie in ruin. The fever has spread globally. America, Europe, Africa, Asia, Australia. It's everywhere, mutating rapidly. Rumours say that the Chinese are close to a cure. But who knows?"

You can offer little news in return. You offer him a pouch full of herbs. "Jim and I have been taking these, and we haven't been sick yet," you explain. "I don't know if they're the reason, but it's worth a try."

And just like that, the man is off. You have a terrible feeling in the pit of your stomach that he's the last healthy person you and Jim will see for a very, very long time. The plague has all but wiped out civilization. You can only hope there are enough healthy people left for the human race to survive.

THE END

To follow another path, turn to page 10.
To learn more about virus outbreaks, turn to page 103.

The fever really kicks in the next day. Tara sets you up in a bed inside the hospital. "We're going to beat this," she says. "I asked Peter to make some calls to get you airlifted out of here."

But no help ever comes. You overhear a few of the students talking late that afternoon.

" ...cases in Mexico, Cuba, Western Europe and Africa. Early reports of the fever spreading in Miami and New York City. Just about every country has sealed its borders. There's nowhere to run."

The disease takes hold fast. You've always been healthy and strong, but your body has no defence against this virus. Still, at first, you fare better than most. You watch as patients around you grow weaker. The death toll reaches 25, then 40. When the wind is right, you can smell the smoke from the fires – the terrible fires where the dead are burned. That evening, Tara sits y your bedside. She's wearing her mask and gloves, but you still feel terrified that you'll infect her.

"I miss home," you tell her. Even the effort of speaking is exhausting. You've been delirious, imagining that you see your friends from home in the room. Once, you could have sworn you spoke to a doctor from your mum's favourite TV series.

"I know," she answers. Her voice quivers. "We'll keep fighting. There's a village not far from here where nobody is ill. There might be something there worth investigating. Peter and I are the only ones still healthy, so I have to go, first thing in the morning."

You nod. It's all the energy you can spare.

"So I won't see you in the morning. I just wanted to … to see you before I go." She doesn't add, "to say goodbye," but you know that's what she means.

"I love you," she says, squeezing your hand.

It's your last memory before falling into a sleep from which you never wake.

THE END

To follow another path, turn to page 10.
To learn more about virus outbreaks, turn to page 103.

You don't like this. Not a bit. "Jim! Run!" you shout, opening your door and bolting towards the road. You run as fast as your feet can carry you, but the sound of another gunshot stops you in your tracks.

You turn in time to see Jim slump to the ground. One of the young men holds a sawn-off shotgun, and he's staring right at you. There's nothing you can do for Jim. All you can do is run.

You run until you can't run any more. You don't care where you're going, just as long as it's away from that gang. Finally, you slump to the ground next to an old concrete building that sits on a terraced slope overlooking the Gulf of Gonâve. The building is cracked and abandoned – probably a victim of the terrible earthquake that struck Haiti in 2010. But that means nobody is around, and right now, that's a good thing.

Turn the page

53

The sea looks so peaceful. But the scene around you is far from it. Smoke rises from dozens of fires scattered around the city. In the distance, you can hear gunfire. The streets are all but deserted. Those who haven't caught the fever have shut themselves in.

That's when it hits you. You're lost and alone in a city crumbling from a plague unlike anything the modern world has ever encountered. You have no food, water or money. You have no way back to Tara, much less back to your home. Even if you survive the streets and find food and water, you won't survive the plague. Not if you stay here.

You stare out at the water and it hits you. *The marina*. Your grandfather taught you a little about sailing. You stand up, brush yourself off and head towards the marina. The few people you encounter along the way steer clear of you.

Most of the boats you see are far too big for you to handle alone. But there, tucked away near the shore, you spot it. A laser-style boat – small and perfect for a single sailor. You climb aboard, cut the boat free and head for open water as quickly as you can. The sooner you're out of Port au Prince and away from civilization, the better.

The waves lap against the hull of your boat as the city grows smaller in the distance. You scan the horizon. The Caribbean is full of small islands and atolls. Maybe, just maybe, you can find somewhere safe to wait out the virus. It won't be easy, but you've escaped Haiti already. You have to believe that you'll be resourceful enough to overcome the obstacles ahead.

THE END

To follow another path, turn to page 10.
To learn more about virus outbreaks, turn to page 103.

Jim's probably right. They're looking for supplies, and your Jeep makes a perfect target. You crane your neck to watch as Jim steps from the Jeep and raises his hands above his head. He shouts something in French.

The gunshot that rings out is deafening. At first, you hardly believe what you're seeing. Jim slumps to the ground. The gang, at least a dozen young men, is on you. You scream and lunge to lock the driver's door, but you're not quick enough. One of the young men, his face glistening in sweat and covered in fever blisters, throws the door open.

You scream again and kick as the men drag you from the car. You desperately try to break free but have no success. You bite and claw as they throw you roughly to the ground. You refuse to flinch when one of them levels a sawn-off shotgun at your head. You should have run when you had the chance.

THE END
To follow another path, turn to page 10.
To learn more about virus outbreaks, turn to page 103.

"The villagers need you here," you tell Tara, holding her arm. "With Jim gone, the hospital is already short-handed. They can't spare you, too. I can run into the city, see if there's any sign of Jim's Jeep. Just tell me where he usually goes for supplies. I can be there and back before sunset."

Tara shakes her head. "No, you're too young to go."

"Don't be ridiculous. This is an emergency. I know how to ride and I'll be careful."

Tara finally gives in. You pack a rucksack and climb onto the rusty old motorbike. Soon you're rumbling down an all but deserted motorway.

As you ride into Port au Prince, the gravity of the situation hits you. The city lies in ruin. Fires burn everywhere. A haze of smoke hangs over the city. You pull a T-shirt from your rucksack and wrap it around your face.

You glance at the crude map Tara has drawn for you. There's a supermarket a kilometre off the motorway. But as you take the exit, you see several cars blocking the road. It isn't until you're right beside them that you realize that one of them is Jim's Jeep. It's completely gutted. What the looters haven't taken, the fire has destroyed. You shiver as you see a series of holes – bullet holes – on the driver's door.

"Jim!" you shout. But you know it's useless. If he survived, he'll be long gone by now.

There's nothing more for you here. You start to turn the motorbike around to head back when you hear a man shout out. You don't need much French to know that you're being ordered to stop.

The voice comes from behind you. You spin and see two men. One holds a shotgun, and it's aimed right at you.

Turn the page

The other man steps forward and forces you from the motorbike. He's covered in blood blisters, and beads of sweat run down his face. He sneers at you, then sneezes. Disgusted and scared, you turn and run.

The streets of Port au Prince are filthy. Dead bodies lie scattered along the roads. Feral dogs roam from abandoned building to abandoned building. You chase them out of a burned-out tin shack and slump to the ground.

You're stuck here. You speak very little French, have no money and can't make it back to Tara. And based on what you've seen at the camp, you'll start showing symptoms of Blood Fever as early as tomorrow.

You drop your head into your hands and sob. One thought keeps repeating in your head: *Why didn't I just go home?*

THE END

To follow another path, turn to page 10.
To learn more about virus outbreaks, turn to page 103.

From everything you've read, the virus seems serious. It would be foolish for you to stay here knowing you could catch it. With a sigh, you agree to turn around and go back home.

After a long, disappointing flight and a restless night's sleep, you're back at home. You go to the cinema with your friends, you spend an afternoon playing tennis, and you start reading a new book. Life seems perfectly normal.

But the news from the Caribbean tells a different story. One evening after dinner, the TV shows images from the Dominican Republic. Field hospitals are overflowing. You watch the headlines at the bottom of the screen:

More than 300 dead in the Dominican Republic ... Outbreaks in Haiti, Puerto Rico, Cuba reaching critical levels ... World Health Organization describes virus as "alarming" ... Recent scares in Miami, Houston and Madrid have millions fleeing the cities ...

Turn the page

By Tuesday – just four days after your return – the news is plastered with stories of Blood Fever in North America, Europe and Northern Africa. News readers and journalists seem really worried. The virus is spreading at rates never before seen.

A week later, you're at home alone when you hear the sirens. As you head outside to see what's happening, the phone rings. It's your dad. He and your mum were visiting your aunt, and you know from his tone that the news is bad. "We're stuck in traffic," he says. "Nothing is moving. There are emergency vehicles everywhere. It's Blood Fever. It's here. We'll be home as soon as we can. Until then, stay inside."

Your mind is racing. What are you supposed to do? You've seen enough disaster films to know that food and water are always the first priority. Perhaps you should stock up before things get out of hand. Or maybe the best idea is to lock the doors and keep away from people.

To stay at home, turn to page 64.
To go and get supplies, turn to page 66.

Everything you've heard about Blood Fever says that it's more contagious than anything people have ever seen. You shut the windows, lock the doors and plop down onto the couch. An hour passes, then two. Finally, the phone rings again.

"Sorry," says your dad. "I don't think we're going to make it home. They're closing off the motorway. We'll get a hotel room tonight and try again tomorrow."

Alone and growing more frightened by the moment, you decide to watch the news. It's almost impossible to believe. More than 100,000 dead already, and that number is growing so fast that nobody seems to know what's going to happen. The governments of the Dominican Republic and Haiti are in full collapse. People are fleeing cities everywhere.

And it's no longer happening just on your TV screen. Sirens echo through the night. No one is out on the streets. You try to call your dad the next morning, but all the lines are busy.

Another day passes with no word from your parents. You're terrified to leave the house. You don't speak to a single soul. Huge clouds of thick black smoke climb into the sky. The water from the tap stops flowing, and the lights flicker for several moments. Perhaps most frightening of all, you no longer hear any sirens. You're feeling depressed and scared as you switch off the TV and climb into bed.

That night the sound of shattering glass wakes you from your shallow sleep. You sit up, hands shaking. Then you hear footsteps and voices. "Take it," rasps a man's voice. "Everything you can find. Take it all." You're being robbed!

To hide, turn to page 68.
To confront the robbers, turn to page 89.

You ride your bike to a local supermarket. The place is swamped with people. A huge spray-painted sign at the entrance reads: "NO HOARDING PLEASE!" But people seem to be ignoring it. One woman rushes past you pushing a shopping trolley full of bottled water and tinned food. She looks at you and slows down.

"Go now," she tells you. "There's not much left, and people are starting to become aggressive. Take anything you can get!"

With that, she runs to her car with the trolley. People are streaming in and out of the shop, carrying all kinds of boxes, bottles and bags. You wonder if there can be much left at all.

That's when you hear the screaming. The situation is going downhill fast. People are panicking. You've got to act now.

To risk going inside the supermarket to get supplies,
turn to page 71.
To try your luck somewhere else, turn to page 75.

Carefully, you slip out of bed, tiptoe across your bedroom floor and crawl into the back of your wardrobe. You listen to the clanging sounds from below and shiver with fear. Everything is going wrong so quickly!

The minutes drag on until all you hear is your own rapid breathing. Finally, you feel safe enough to climb out and creep downstairs. It's silent – they've gone.

You groan as you look at the kitchen. Shattered glass and plates litter the floor. The fridge and cupboards are empty, and they took anything of value. You slump to the floor and put your head down.

That's when you hear shouting outside. You peer out of the window and see flames licking the outer wall of the house next door! *Oh no! Mrs Thomas!*

Mrs Thomas is 85 years old and lives alone in that house. The flames climb up the outer walls and rise along the rooftop. Your houses are only a few metres apart. The blaze is sure to spread to your house!

To gather everything you can from your own house before the fire spreads, turn to page 72.
To rush to help Mrs Thomas, turn to page 83.

It's now or never. You park your bike and shove your way inside. You're shocked by what you see. People are scooping up handfuls of goods and running out of the shop. You see two women fighting over a trolley. Several employees are trying to maintain order, but the hoarding has turned into looting.

The cereal aisle is just in front of you. The shelves have been ransacked. Open cereal boxes lie everywhere. Spilled cereal crunches beneath your feet. You spot a bag of granola under some rubbish and grab it.

Over the next several chaotic minutes, you manage to grab several tins of beans, some tomato soup and a bag of peanuts. You carry it all in a cloth shopping bag. The chaos is growing worse by the moment. It's time to get out while you still can.

To get out now without paying, turn to page 74.
To attempt to pay for your shopping, turn to page 87.

For all you know, Mrs Thomas isn't even at home. It would be foolish to rush next door.

Your mind races. You know you only have minutes to grab what you can. You rush into your room, throw open your top drawer and grab the envelope full of cash that you've saved. You shove it into your rucksack, along with some clothes, a Swiss-army knife your dad gave you, a family photo and a spare T-shirt that you can wrap around your face as a mask. You're zipping up the bag when the house's smoke detectors begin their shrill screaming. Time's up!

You throw your rucksack over your shoulder and dart onto the landing. Already the smoke is thickening. You bound down the stairs, out the door and onto the street. As you move, you see three dark figures in the distance.

There's no time to stick around. You slide around the side of the house to where you keep your bike, climb on, and begin to pedal as fast as you can. Only when you're several kilometres away do you stop to catch your breath.

What are you supposed to do now? Your home is gone. The town has fallen into chaos. Half the people are sick and dying. And many others seem to have gone crazy. Is anywhere safe? Your aunt and uncle live about 50 kilometres away. But is there any reason to believe the situation there is better? Would you be better off just finding somewhere far from people and waiting out the crisis?

To head for your aunt and uncle's house, turn to page 80.
To find somewhere in the woods to wait out the crisis, turn to page 98.

You don't believe in stealing. But as you scan the supermarket, you realize that nobody is there to even take your money. The only assistant you can see appears to be busy cramming supplies into her own bag! You'd seen images of looting on the news. But you never thought it would happen *here*! It's time to leave before looting turns into full-scale rioting. You breathe a sigh of relief as you step outside and climb on your bike.

Your mind races as you pedal your bike away from the shop. You can hardly believe that this is happening where you live! People are panicking, and everything is starting to break down. Blood Fever is bad, but it seems at this point that the panic might be even worse.

Lost in your thoughts, it takes a few minutes before you notice the rising smoke. You're only a little way from your home when you see it. The blaze covers your entire street! Several people are running from the scene. You recognize a neighbour, crying, clinging to a photo album.

Turn the page

76

By the time firefighters arrive, it's too late. At least seven homes have been completely destroyed – including your own. Smoke rises in several other parts of town. You hear distant sirens.

The days that follow are a blur. At first, you're taken to a makeshift shelter at your school. But one night it all gets too much. People everywhere, coughing, sneezing. Staying there seems like a death sentence. You try a friend's house, but no one answers when you knock. You spend the night alone in your friend's garden shed.

Turn the page

Meanwhile, the situation gets worse by the hour. The bodies of the dead pile up in the streets. Even worse is the smell of the fires where people are burning the bodies. In a matter of weeks, your nice, modern town has fallen into what feels like the Dark Ages.

You keep your distance from people as best you can. It's not hard to do. Nobody seems to want to get close. The few conversations you do have are shouted from a distance. The rumour is that the army has set up a refugee camp several towns away. You've still got your bike – the only really useful possession you have. You can't keep living on the street, so you begin the journey.

About halfway there, you spot another person about your age on a scooter. From across the street, you greet each other.

"Hey," he calls. "Are you healthy?" You nod. "Thought so. I can spot a sick one a mile away. My name's Ben. Me and some other kids have set up camp outside town. It's just an old abandoned church. But we're all healthy, and we're working together to get through this. I think you'd fit right in. Do you want to join us?"

To join Ben's group, turn to page 90.
To continue to the refugee camp, turn to page 96.

It's clear that your parents aren't coming home. You don't know if they're alive or dead. You're a teenager in a world gone mad. What you need is family. You tug the straps of your rucksack tight and begin the long ride.

It's an eerie midnight ride. The roads are deserted. Yet as you ride past homes and boarded-up businesses, you hear the occasional distant scream. At one point, you watch as several helicopters speed overhead. They look military, but it's hard to be sure in the dark.

Dawn is breaking when you arrive at the bridge that leads into your aunt and uncle's town. You hear shouting in the distance. As you pedal, you see a huge crowd of people spilling into the street. People are screaming, throwing things. A teenage boy rides a scooter in your direction. "Are you ill?" he shouts. You shake your head.

Turn the page

"Don't go that way then. It's a hot zone. Everyone there'll be dead in a week."

"What about you?" you ask.

"Not ill. Not yet, at least. I'm just out trying to find supplies, but I'll have to look somewhere else."

The boy, Ben, is living in a camp outside the town with a group of other kids. They were part of a scouting group when the plague struck. Now they're living in an abandoned church. "You're welcome to join us," he says, looking you up and down and seeing no signs of illness. "If you want to."

To follow Ben, turn to page 90.
To take your chances in town, turn to page 93.

You sprint down the stairs and through the doorway. You leap over the hedges and throw open the door to Mrs Thomas' house. Smoke pours out of the doorway.

"Mrs Thomas!" you shout, pulling your T-shirt up to cover your mouth and nose. "Are you in here?"

"Help me!" you hear. It's coming from the kitchen. You rush inside, squinting because the smoke stings your eyes. Mrs Thomas is lying on the floor. There's blood on her face, and she's coughing violently.

"Come on, we have to get you out of here!" The woman groans with pain as you help her to her feet. She leans against you as you help her out of the house. You move her across the street, away from the fire, until you both collapse onto a neighbour's lawn.

"Help us!" you shout. You're afraid Mrs Thomas might not make it. Just then you see a military jeep rumbling down the road.

Turn the page

"You!" shouts a man dressed in a military uniform. You can't see his face, as it's covered by an elaborate mask. "We saw the flames. Is everyone all right?"

"Yes. I think so," you tell the man, an army captain called Taylor. A paramedic takes a blood sample from you and places it inside a test unit. As he waits, the medic examines Mrs Thomas. "She's in a bad way," says the medic. "She would recover from her injuries. But … she's got it. She's infected. Take her to Holding Camp 7."

"What does that mean, Captain?" you ask, panic creeping into your voice.

Captain Taylor gives you a sad look. "She's going to a camp for the infected," he answers. At that moment, the little testing unit beeps. A green light blinks on the display.

"Your sample is clean. You're not infected. So you'll be going north, to the mountains. The virus doesn't seem to like high altitude. We're moving people there while our scientists work on a cure."

Turn the page

You feel a sense of relief wash over you. "Hold on a second, Captain," says the medic before turning to you. "Have you just carried this woman out of her burning house?"

You nod. Behind you, you can hear Mrs Thomas' hacking cough.

The medic looks at Captain Taylor and shakes his head. Your heart sinks as it hits you. Mrs Thomas is infected. You carried her, coughing and bleeding, out of her house. That means you're infected now, too.

The captain gives you a long, sad look. "Sorry. It was a brave thing you did there. I wish there was something I could do." He turns and shouts. "We've got two infected for transport!"

And with that, you're off to a camp for the infected. You know that, unless there's a miracle, it's where you'll spend the final days of your life.

THE END

To follow another path, turn to page 10.
To learn more about virus outbreaks, turn to page 103.

Just because others are stealing, that doesn't make it right. With your bag in hand, you stride up to the customer service counter, where a woman is frantically trying to telephone for help.

"Can I pay for this here?" you shout.

The woman gives you a strange look, as if she doesn't quite believe what you're asking. Just then, a young man steps up behind you. "Please," he says, coughing into his sleeve. "I need help. I've got two little ones at home, and someone broke in and took all of our food!" The assistant barely seems to notice. She's grabbing supplies from behind the counter.

The man grabs at your shoulder. "Help me! Please!" A shiver traces your spine as you look at the man. His face is covered in blisters. His hands feel warm through the material of your T-shirt. You back away, thrusting the bag at the man. "Take it," you shout, willing to do anything to get away from him. You run out of the shop and pedal home as fast as you can.

Turn the page

The symptoms begin two days later. You're on the sofa, shivering, clutching a bucket in case you need to vomit. You try to follow the news on the TV, but your attention wanders. Entire cities are burning. Governments are collapsing all around the world. There's talk of an experimental treatment, but nobody seems to have any details.

Desperate, you climb on your bike and start riding towards the hospital. You have to stop once to be sick in a bush, but you somehow manage to make it. Sadly, you find no help there. Hundreds of people crowd around the building. There isn't a bed to spare. One elderly man explains to you that most of the doctors have fallen ill themselves.

It was your last hope. You look around and see death everywhere. You know that, unless there's a miracle, that will be your fate as well.

THE END
To follow another path, turn to page 10.
To learn more about virus outbreaks, turn to page 103.

Someone is in your house stealing your food and supplies! Your blood boils at the thought. You scan your room for a weapon. Propped against the wall is a cricket bat – perfect.

Clutching the bat, you creep down the hallway. You hear two voices and crashing noises as the burglars pull things out of your cabinets. Rounding the corner into the kitchen, you raise the bat above your head and shout "STOP!"

Two men, dressed all in black, are loading tinned food into a large sack. For a moment, they look shocked. But that soon passes.

"Put the bag down and get out of my house," you stammer. You try your hardest to sound strong, but your voice wavers and cracks.

"Bad idea," says one of the men as he pulls a knife from his waistband. You don't even have time to swing your bat.

THE END

To follow another path, turn to page 10.
To learn more about virus outbreaks, turn to page 103.

You have nowhere to go. It's an easy decision. You turn your bike around and follow Ben out of town, turning off on a small country lane. After a few kilometres, he points out the abandoned church.

"It's not much to look at, but it keeps the rain and wind off of us."

There are twelve other people there, all about your age. Some carry water from a nearby well. Others collect wood for the fire. One girl is preparing a meal from their limited supplies.

"We reckon things will get worse before they get better," Ben says, introducing you to the others as you pass by. Most seem friendly, once they're assured that you don't have the virus. "We'll wait it out, relying on each other to get through it. There's strength in numbers."

Turn the page

And so the group becomes your new family. Over the next few months, you live and work together, keeping away from the rest of civilization as much as you can. You help to operate the group's long-range radio, monitoring the news as best you can.

The world is falling apart. According to the radio, as many as 95 per cent of the world's people are dead. But as the months crawl by, Blood Fever wanes. The survivors have finally developed an immunity to the virus. Soon it will be time to leave your safe home and rebuild. It will be a long and painful process, but you're just grateful that you're alive to have the chance. One day, you'll set out to search for your parents and friends. But for now, you're safe.

THE END

To follow another path, turn to page 10.
To learn more about virus outbreaks, turn to page 103.

"I need to find my aunt and uncle," you tell the boy, waving as you begin to pedal. He gives you a disappointed look, shrugs his shoulders and heads the other way.

The streets are madness. You try to slip by quietly, but it's no good. Several people turn towards you. You hear a woman's voice shout, "A bike! Get it!"

You turn and try to pedal hard. But something slams into your bike from behind. Your back tyre skids on the road. You react quickly to right your balance, but then someone is grabbing you. More hands pull you down. "No! Leave me alone! Stop!" you cry. But no one is listening.

The rush is on. People are fighting and clawing at each other, trying to get your bike. A man grabs your rucksack from your shoulder, yanking it so hard that the strap snaps. You reach out and grab at the other strap, but the man turns and kicks you hard in the shoulder. Your arm goes numb from the pain and drops to the ground.

Turn the page

In time, the mob moves on. You lie in the road, bleeding and in pain. Your shoulder is either badly sprained or broken, and you can't put weight on one of your ankles. Worse still, everything you owned has been taken.

An old woman stands over you. "You weren't infected" she says. You shake your head. She gives you a sad look. "You are now. Sorry, child."

You know she's right. Blood Fever is so contagious that just being near someone who has the virus is likely to infect you. And you've just faced a mob.

You'll be feeling the first symptoms soon. You know that there's nowhere you can go for help. If your aunt and uncle aren't infected already, you can't expose them. You wish you'd stayed with Tara. At least then, you'd have been with family.

THE END
To follow another path, turn to page 10.
To learn more about virus outbreaks, turn to page 103.

You don't know this boy, and you're not about to trust a stranger with your life. "Thanks for the offer. I've got somewhere to be."

Ben shrugs, then he's off. You ride through the day and into the night. By the time you see the camp in the distance, you're hungry, dehydrated and exhausted.

The camp sits behind a tall fence. You approach the gate, guarded by a trio of armed military police. "I need help," you tell them.

They look you over, then look at each other. "Infected," one of them whispers.

"No! I'm not ill, I swear it." You realize how you must look. You're thin and pale from lack of sleep, food and water. Your hair is matted, and your face is dirty. You're drenched in sweat from the long ride.

"All right then," says one of the MPs, backing away. "We'll set you up in a nice spot straight away."

The MP straps on a mask and leads you inside. Immediately you're led inside a building, down a flight of stairs and along an underground tunnel. Men and women wearing bright yellow biohazard suits come and go.

"They'll take care of you in here," says the MP. In the room, rows of sick beds contain people coughing, vomiting … dying. You spin and shout "No!" as the heavy metal door locks shut behind you.

An intercom sounds. "Please select a bed. A doctor will be with you shortly."

You slump to the floor. You weren't infected, but now you certainly are. And you know that means you'll never be leaving.

THE END

To follow another path, turn to page 10.
To learn more about virus outbreaks, turn to page 103.

Being around people isn't safe. Even the healthy people are a danger now. That means you've only got one option. You tighten the straps on your rucksack and begin to ride. You've already got a place in mind. Your parents take you camping sometimes in a nearby national park. If they're still alive and healthy, perhaps they'll find you there. It's a long shot, but you'll take it.

You get there just before dawn. It's deserted. The reflection of the sunrise on the smooth water almost makes you forget the madness you just left behind.

A week passes. You're grateful for the outdoor skills your parents taught you. You've made yourself a crude shelter, built a fire pit, collected and boiled drinking water and even caught some fish. If not for the dark plumes of smoke in the distant sky, you might be able to imagine it was all a bad dream.

Turn the page

Another week goes by. You can't stand not knowing. So you hike down to where you hid your bike. There's a small town a few kilometres up the road.

As you pedal your bike into town, you know things are still very wrong. The streets seem to be empty. Doors and windows are boarded up. It feels like a ghost town.

That's when the shot rings out. The bullet clangs off a postbox not 3 metres from where you're standing.

"We don't want any trouble!" shouts a voice. It's a woman. You can see her in the window of one of the buildings that lines the street.

"I'm not infected!" you shout back, holding your arms out to your side.

"Don't care. Just go back the way you came. Like I said, we don't want trouble. But I'll shoot you if I have to."

You don't have much choice. You back away, climb onto your bike and pedal off.

That night, in front of your campfire, you smile. That didn't go well. But now you know people are surviving. The virus will run its course. You're sure of that. And then it will be time to rebuild. All you have to do is keep yourself alive until then. It will be a long, difficult process, but you're certain you can do it.

You reflect as you stare into the dancing flames of your fire. You've lost so much – your home, your family, your friends. But you're alive and healthy. You have a chance, and you won't let it slip away.

THE END

To follow another path, turn to page 10.
To learn more about virus outbreaks, turn to page 103.

THREATS FROM WITHIN:
PANDEMICS OF PAST AND PRESENT

Blood Fever isn't real, but throughout history, people have waged an unending battle with diseases. Many illnesses, such as the common cold, aren't much more than a nuisance to otherwise healthy people. But once in a while, a disease appears that wreaks havoc on the human body. These diseases can kill and spread at alarming rates. Entire cities, countries and continents can be affected. This is known as a pandemic, or plague.

For many, the word *plague* brings to mind one of the most deadly diseases known to humans. The Black Death, or Bubonic Plague, struck Europe during the 1300s. The plague may have originated in Asia, but nobody knows exactly when it began or where it came from.

The bacteria that caused the Black Death killed as many as 75 million people. This deadly disease devastated Europe, killing up to two-thirds of its population. Historians estimate that when the disease reached England in 1348, it killed between one third and one half of the population in a matter of months.

In the late 1400s and early 1500s, Europeans sailed across the Atlantic Ocean to North America. They brought with them many diseases, such as measles, smallpox and scarlet fever. Europeans had developed immunity to these diseases. Their bodies knew how to fight them. But the Native Americans had no such defences. The diseases ripped through native populations, wiping out entire nations. Experts estimate that as many as 20 million Native Americans died, mainly from smallpox. That figure may have represented 95 per cent of the native population.

Recent outbreaks such as AIDS, swine flu and Ebola prove that plagues are not just a thing of the past. Many people remain confident that modern medicine and science can fight most diseases.

Others aren't convinced. Diseases have shown they can adapt to even the strongest medicines. Many bacterial diseases were once easily cured with antibiotics. But over time, these bacteria have mutated. The diseases have become resistant to drugs. It's proof that the battle between medicine and disease is ongoing and, perhaps, never-ending.

It's not just mutated diseases that are the problem. New threats of disease – both those that are natural and those created in laboratories – are always arising. Today, a person can travel halfway around the world in a matter of hours. That gives diseases the chance to spread at rates that were impossible in the past. What would happen if a new deadly disease spread so quickly that even modern medicine could not keep up? Could such a devastating plague really occur? Agencies such as the World Health Organization (WHO) work to keep the threat to a minimum.

SURVIVAL REFERENCE GUIDE

If a terrible virus ever threatened to wipe out humanity, you'd need every advantage to survive. In this story, there was little warning. But in real life, we might have weeks or even months to prepare before the worst of the plague. What sort of items might you gather to maximize your chances of survival? Here's a suggested survival kit!

SURVIVAL KIT

*A face mask or surgical mask

*Hand sanitizer

*Disinfectants such as surgical spirit

*A first-aid kit including lots of sterile bandages

*A battery-operated short-wave radio with plenty of batteries

*A small power generator or solar panels

*Reference books and survival guides (the internet may not be available)

*Torches

*Tinned or dehydrated food

*Bottled water and water purification tablets

*A few good books – you may be spending a lot of time alone!

TEN THINGS TO REMEMBER DURING A PANDEMIC

- **Don't shake hands.** It might seem rude, but a handshake is like public transport for a virus. Choose a polite nod and wave instead.

- **Hospitals aren't really sterile.** Hospitals might seem like extremely clean, sterile places. But they're really crawling with germs. Go to the hospital only when you really need to.

- **One may be the loneliest number, but it's also the safest.** People are social creatures. We crave the company of others. But during an outbreak, isolation is your best chance of survival. Keep your contact with others to a bare minimum.

- **Be informed.** That means reading newspapers and keeping up with the news on the radio, TV or internet. Pay attention to what's going on. There's no substitute for knowledge.

- **Wash, wash and wash again**. Your number one defence against infection is clean hands. Every time you touch a door handle, light switch or anything in public, you're risking getting viruses or bacteria on your hands. From there, it's a short trip to your mouth, nose or eyes. Wash frequently. Use soap and hand sanitizer.

- **Cover your sneezes and coughs.** If you become ill, a cough or sneeze can be like a virus-spewing bomb. Sneeze into a tissue and keep your germs to yourself!

- **Looks can be deceiving.** People don't appear to be ill the moment they catch a virus. It usually takes a couple of days. Just because someone *looks* healthy doesn't mean they aren't infected.

- **Stock up.** As soon as a pandemic starts, stock up on essentials. Every trip out to the shops is a risk. If you've got supplies for a week or two, you can stay safely locked away in your own home.

- **Know the warning signs.** Most diseases have tell-tale signs. Whether it's coughing, sneezing, fever or blisters, know the early signs of an infection. Early treatment can be the difference between life and death.

- **Desperate people do desperate things.** Most people in the world are basically good, but in desperate situations it is human nature to look out first for ourselves and our families. During an outbreak, you might have to be extra cautious around people you don't know.

GLOSSARY

ANTI-VIRAL medicine that helps the body fight off viral infections

CONTAGIOUS easily spread and having a high rate of infection

DEHYDRATED lacking water in the body

DELIRIOUS disturbed state of mind; people suffering from delirium may think they see people and things that aren't really there

HOARD stockpile valuable supplies

IMMUNITY body's natural defence against a disease

INFECT cause someone to catch a disease

LOOT steal from shops or houses during a riot, war or other disaster

MUTATE change in form; as viruses mutate, they can become more difficult to treat

PANDEMIC outbreak of a disease that infects large numbers of people worldwide

PLAGUE uncontrolled outbreak of a deadly disease

PYRE large pile of wood or other material that can be burned, often used for burning dead bodies

STERILE clean and free of micro-organisms such as bacteria

VACCINATE protect someone against disease by introducing his or her immune system to a dead or dormant virus or bacteria

READ MORE

The Soterion Mission, Stewart Ross (Curious Fox, 2013)

Super-Plague (A World After...), Anne Rooney (Raintree, 2013)

WEBSITES

www.bbc.co.uk/history/british/middle_ages/
Learn more about the Black Death.

**www.booktrust.org.uk/books/teenagers/writing-tips/
writing-fiction**
Have a go at writing your own virus outbreak stories using some of these top tips!

AUTHOR

Matt Doeden is the author of more than 200 children's fiction and non-fiction books. A lifelong fan of science fiction and "what if" stories, he lives in Minnesota, USA, with his wife and two children.

ILLUSTRATOR

A native of Yorkshire, Stewart Johnson began freelancing as an illustrator in 1986. He originally started illustrating for the RPG market before moving into comics. His first jobs were with publishers Fleetway and Marvel UK. He left the comics field for two years for a job in advertising before returning in 1993 to work for US publishers DC Comics & Marvel Comics. He is married with two daughters.